THE
LION KING

This special edition was printed for Kohl's Department Stores, Inc. (for distribution on behalf of Kohl's Cares, LLC, its wholly owned subsidiary), by Disney Press, New York/Los Angeles.

Kohl's
1204165-00
123387
07/14–08/14

Printed in China
First Edition
1 3 5 7 9 10 8 6 4 2
ISBN 978-1-4847-2160-5
G615-7693-2-14182

For more Disney Press fun, visit www.disneybooks.com

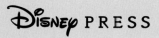

DISNEY PRESS

New York • Los Angeles

The hot African sun rose over the plains. It was a special day for the animals of the Pride Lands. That day they would celebrate the birth of King Mufasa's son, Simba.

A line of mighty elephants thundered across the dry ground, trumpeting with joy. Cheetahs and zebras followed. Brightly colored birds soared above them, swooping and turning on the breeze. No one, from the smallest ant to the tallest giraffe, wanted to miss such an important moment!

High above on Pride Rock, King Mufasa and Queen Sarabi watched as Rafiki, the wise baboon, presented their newborn son to the kingdom.

The animals cheered and bowed before Prince Simba.

But not everyone was happy about the birth of a new prince. In a cave at the back side of Pride Rock, a scraggly lion with a dark mane paced back and forth. This was Scar, the king's brother.

Scar had just caught a mouse when Zazu, the king's advisor, appeared at the doorway to the cave. He was there to warn Scar that Mufasa was coming to see him.

"Sarabi and I didn't see you at the presentation of Simba," Mufasa said when he appeared.

"You are the king's brother," Zazu said. "You should have been first in line."

"I was first in line, until the little hairball was born," Scar growled. And with a snap of his jaws, Scar stalked out of the cave.

Simba grew into a strong cub. Early one morning, he and Mufasa climbed to the top of Pride Rock.

"Look, Simba," Mufasa said. "Everything the light touches is our kingdom."

Simba scanned the horizon and noticed a dark spot in the distance. "What about that shadowy place?" he asked.

"That's beyond our borders. You must never go there," Mufasa answered.

Later, as Simba headed home, he ran into Scar.

"Hey, Uncle Scar!" he shouted. "Guess what! My dad just showed me the whole kingdom!"

Scar looked slyly at the young cub. "He didn't show you what's beyond that rise at the northern border?"

"Well, no. He said I can't go there," Simba answered.

"And he's absolutely right," Scar said. "An elephant graveyard is no place for a young prince."

Simba thought an elephant graveyard sounded like an amazing place to visit! He couldn't wait to find his best friend, Nala, and tell her all about it.

When Simba returned home, he found Nala visiting with Sarabi. "Can Nala and I go and play?" Simba asked.

Sarabi agreed, as long as Zazu went with the cubs.

Soon Simba and Nala were racing across the Pride Lands. They led Zazu through herds of animals until they lost him. Finally, they arrived at the Elephant Graveyard.

Suddenly, three hyenas slithered out of an elephant skull. Just as they were about to attack the young cubs, Mufasa appeared and sent them flying. The hyenas slinked away, and Mufasa glared at Simba.

"I'm very disappointed in you!" he told his son. "You deliberately disobeyed me!"

Simba peered up at his father. "I was just trying to be brave, like you," he said.

"Being brave doesn't mean you go looking for trouble," Mufasa answered.

"Dad, we're pals, right? And we'll always be together, right?" Simba asked.

Mufasa looked up at the stars. "Simba, let me tell you something that my father told me. Look at the stars. The great kings of the past look down on us from those stars. So whenever you feel alone, just remember that those kings will always be there to guide you. And so will I."

The following day, Scar invited Simba to join him in the gorge. "Now you wait here," he told his nephew. "Your father has a marvelous surprise for you."

Leaving the young prince alone, Scar signaled the hyenas, who chased a herd of wildebeests into the gorge.

From a distance, Mufasa noticed the rising dust. Suddenly, Scar appeared at his side. "Stampede! In the gorge!" he shouted. "Simba's down there!"

Mufasa plunged into the gorge. He quickly found Simba and helped him onto a nearby ledge. But there were too many wildebeests, and Mufasa was knocked back into the stampede.

"Brother, help me!" he shouted to Scar. But Scar just watched Mufasa fall.

Later, when the animals had passed, Simba stood over his father's body. "It was an accident. I didn't mean for it to happen," he cried. "What am I going to do?"

Scar stood behind him. "Run away, Simba. Run! Run away and never return."

Simba ran as fast as he could. Scar's hyenas chased after him, over a cliff and through a thorny patch of brambles. Finally, Simba escaped. He was on his own in the hot, dry desert.

The young prince walked as far as he could, until finally he collapsed.

When Simba awoke, he found himself in a grassy, shaded jungle. In front of him stood a meerkat named Timon and a warthog named Pumbaa. The two animals had found Simba in the desert and brought him to their home.

Timon asked Simba where he had come from, but Simba didn't want to talk about his past.

"Take my advice, kid," Timon said. "You've gotta put your past behind you. No past, no future, no worries—*hakuna matata*."

Time passed and Simba grew up.

One day, as Pumbaa was walking through the jungle, a lioness appeared and began to chase him. She was about to attack him when Simba came to his rescue.

As Simba wrestled with the lioness, he recognized her. "Nala?" he asked. "What are you doing here?"

Nala jumped up and began to nuzzle Simba. The two lions were happy to have found each other.

That evening, Simba went for a walk alone. Nala wanted him to go back to the Pride Lands, but Simba knew he couldn't challenge Scar.

Suddenly, Rafiki appeared in front of him. "Who are you?" Simba asked the baboon.

"I know who you are," Rafiki answered. "Mufasa's boy."

Simba told Rafiki that his father was dead, but the wise baboon disagreed. "He's alive, and I'll show him to you."

Rafiki told Simba to look into the pond in front of him.

Simba looked down and saw a lion in the water. "That's not my father," he said. "It's just my reflection."

"Look harder," Rafiki told him. "You see, he lives in you."

Rafiki touched the water and Simba's reflection turned into the face of his father.

Suddenly, the clouds shifted. Simba looked up and gasped. Mufasa's form had magically appeared in the sky.

"Look inside yourself, Simba," his father said. "You are more than what you have become. You must take your place in the Circle of Life."

Simba knew his father was right. It was time for him to return to the Pride Lands and claim his rightful place as king.

But the Pride Lands were not as Simba had left them. Scar was letting the hyenas run wild, and there was no food or water.

"We must leave Pride Rock," Sarabi told Scar.

Scar refused to listen. "We're not going anywhere," he told her. "*I am the king.*"

Suddenly, Scar heard a low growl. Lightning flashed, and the lion pack saw Simba standing atop Pride Rock.

● ● ● ● ● ● ● ● ● ● ●

Scar jumped back. He was surprised, but he was not going to let Simba reclaim the kingdom without a fight.

As Scar spoke with Simba, he tricked him into telling the lionesses that he had caused Mufasa's death.

Scar smirked. "Oh, Simba, you're in trouble again. But this time Daddy isn't here to save you. And now everybody knows why."

As the lionesses murmured about Simba's confession, Scar attacked the young prince, backing him over a cliff.

Scar looked over the edge of the rock at Simba.

"Now *this* looks familiar," he said. "This is how your father looked just before I killed him!"

Hearing the terrible truth about his father, Simba summoned the extra strength he needed to lunge at Scar.

"Please, Simba," Scar pleaded with his nephew. "I'll make it up to you. I promise. How can I prove myself?"

"Run. Run away, Scar, and never return," Simba answered. Scar started to slink off, but then he turned and lunged one last time at Simba.

Simba moved quickly and flipped Scar over the cliff, where a pack of hyenas was waiting hungrily for him.

Limping badly, Simba climbed up to the very top of Pride Rock. He let out a magnificent roar as he looked over his kingdom.

Before long, the Pride Lands flourished again. Nala stayed by Simba's side, and soon they gave the animals of the Pride Lands a reason to celebrate. The elephants trumpeted, and the zebras stomped their hooves. High above them, Rafiki held up the king and queen's cub. The Pride Lands had a new prince.